Tower Road

Tower Road

DEVOTIONALS

Kaya Black

I fly over oceans to hold you.

Tell me, brother, what happens after death?
The whole world is arguing about it—
Some say you become a ghost,
Others that you go to heaven,
And some that you get close to God,
And the Vedas insist you're a bit of sky
Reflected in a jar fated to shatter.

When you look for sin and virtue in nothing,
You end up with nothing.
The elements live in the body together
But go their own ways at death.

Prasad says: you end, brother,
Where you began, a reflection
Rising in water, mixing with water,
Finally one with water.

—Ramprasad Sen

Grace and Mercy in Her Wild Hair:
Selected Poems to the Mother Goddess

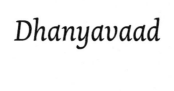

Dhanyavaad

WE WALK WITH THE OVER SOUL, alone at Tower Road beach. Splashing surf. The sun in your hair. I'm laughing. You let me hook an arm in the crook of your elbow. The lake is pristine, the horizon a painting I can almost touch.

You are so present, a breathing dream. I feel the warmth of your skin, your smiles. Your green eyes glisten with the magnificent water.

The sand solidifies into pillars of stone. Crows slice around them; we hop and jump. There are people now, we're in Kolkata. Musical language wafts like birdsong.

At the end of the path is a small, sunny museum. It's flocked with terracotta goddesses and scientific dioramas. We explore. A metal net suspends from the ceiling, filled with steel balls held together by electric current. A sign explains that this is to demonstrate how every choice, every action, affects and interconnects and moves through everything and everyone.

You come up behind me. "Are you learning?" you ask. Your voice is low fire; I evaporate.

Sing through this vessel.
The I's immaterial.
Lives are collections
of sunken shards.
Breakage returns us
to beach sand.

Give me your hand.
There are miracles
under
the water.

Return to the world

"'Return to the world still more brilliant because of your former sorrows.'"   —Alexandre Dumas, *The Count of Monte Cristo*

YOU LIVE IN AN OPULENT MANSION overlooking the sea. Sunlight glints on the immaculate sapphire water. Naked masts of sailboats clink and whisper in the breeze.

The mansion is crammed with people in vibrant colors. Your

haughty wife bulges beneath an auburn wig. Three children carry her, forming a chair with their arms. They wear the servants' black uniform. She barks buoyantly in an oily red dress. No one sees the children. No one sees the servers. Food and drinks float on invisible arms.

Your son and daughter guzzle and gab. I've met your society, know a few stories. But no one really knows me. I am a shadow at the threshold, searching for you. You say our life is private, that I would not care for these people. Yet I have never been loved openly and with pride. I wonder how it would be to be by your side.

You are boisterous in the center. Your hair is utterly white, you wear an extravagant white suit. Our eyes ignite over the crowd and now your focus has changed. I am dark in the doorway in a modest black dress. I try to step towards you. Your gaze does not invite or refuse. I feel adrift. You are the only person that sees me.

"Give me a job," I beg a passing servant. The sun is setting in sharp bronze, your many rooms disintegrating into dusk. If I am not visible, I want to be useful.

"Light the candles," she suggests, harried, not providing any tools.

Candles are everywhere, on tables and mantelpieces, atop bookshelves and trays. I stroke one and it lights. I spread fingers over wicks and they bloom, golden and excited. A murmur sweeps down the path I am creating. I flow through the crowd, tingling and touching tips, raising light and heat and energy. Fire surrounds us in an implacable swirl. They have all become shadows in my incandescent love for you. I do not care if this destroys me. I burn only to illuminate you.

"Whose child? born / before the gods."

—Ursula K Le Guin, *Lao Tzu: Tao Te Ching*

Love is the space that separates. Love allows us to move. *We define presence, profusion, in union.* Flesh intersects, collectives affect. *Love is so vast, it may seem to vanish.* Past comprehension. *Still, we can feel.* Timeless tangible press of connections. *No near or far, respire or die.* No true divide between bodies, earth, sky. *Forever is now, as here as our kiss.* There is no matter and no emptiness.

So let's just say yes....

309 Hallelujah Ave,
Brackenwood

One day it occurs to me to transform humans into trees. I sit on a stone bench, downtown in a wide central square. Gargantuan metal structures pierce the sky. I'm penned in, people everywhere. Millions, billions of electric waves swamp over me. I feel everything.

The book is open in my lap. With your green pen, I write the appropriate words. Page, ink and language are just tools, channels. The energy is within me, terrifying and vast. I cannot fathom the deciding factors: who will remain human, why the rest are chosen. The words quiver and melt, incomprehensible. I do not stop writing. I am merely an instrument myself.

Buildings dissolve into green and brown. Wherever people are, on whatever high floor, their new roots burst through and out and down into the earth. Skyscrapers become dense, monumental copses, glass twinkling like hail. The streets erupt into woods of suddenly shattered cars. Sidewalks fragment into dust. Branches ache upwards. Thick, dark, verdant leaves unfurl, filling the sky with a tiered canopy. Sunlight glitters in a jade haze.

There were once, so recently, so many humans on this planet.

Remnants peek around avenues of trunks. Fear is quickly overcome by wonder. Live television is frantic, beseeching; often, a tree is stolid in the newscaster's seat. I scratch another verse. Zoo cages clang open, echoing.

Phone buzzes in pocket. "How many times must I say it?" you shout. "You are the most important person in my life."

"You said I'd change the landscape," I reply. "Yet everyone is still alive."

Thanks to Adam Phillips.

You are the swift and splendid pause,
the center of each breath.

Bogart Grove

COBBLESTONES. Deepening dusk. Lanterns in iron arabesques. Clattering autumn leaves, shadows melding over amber light. The rustling hush of trees yearning to rest. Wind prickles my face. The lake is nearby, massive and invisible.

I sit on a low concrete post along a decrepit gate. Chains thick as anchors. The train empties; its wail fades into the orange evening. People pour down the mossy street. I face into the flood, peering for your gait, your tie, your eyes. I wear a thin black trench coat, tatty gloves. Brittle leaves sprinkle on the breeze, in my streaming hair.

You stride through the weary masses, and the moon crests solely to brighten you. Your warm wool coat, brown leather briefcase. I hop off the post and stand steadfast, recognizing you instantly. "Why are you here?" you hiss, clutching my elbow. Unknown faces eddy around us.

"I came to meet you." I'm stifling tears. Every cell throbs in response to your resonant presence. I've waited for you for fifteen years. "Please, will you let me in?"

"Fine," you grumble. "Get off the street. You are my interior story."

Brick and greystone buildings commingle in a long, steep row. You guide me up dark steps. Your home is burnished burnt sienna, door and windowsills a lush green. Ivy twines over the walls. I heft your briefcase as you unlock.

The anterooms are sparse. Bare bulbs, rusted folding chairs, a cot. You lead me farther in, through a maze of many doors. Now there are deep winged chairs, oak bookcases, green shade lamps, a generous bed. "Tell no one," you scold. I'm confused by seclusion. Am I already a ghost?

In the heart of a star,

space

between our ages

is not

that far apart.

The Wall

I AM LOST in the opalescent nighttime city. Turquoise gleams from windows, street lamps, taillights. Airy metal towers, perforated glass, skeins of wire. Stone steps lead into dimness, out of darkness. Trolley tracks climb stairs, loop onto sidewalks, weave through streets, up the sides of buildings, teeter on railings, disappear down dismal alleys. The trolley is small, full of empty faces.

Everywhere, in the distance, rising high and thunderously mute between canyons of city, is The Wall. It is solid water. Not a lake, not faraway shoreline. It is a rippling, pulsing wall of water, insurmountable into the sky, gushing, flowing, but firm, still. Every lantern and pane reflects its emerald glow. I do not know if the sun seeps through.

I am searching for you. Clanking down fire escapes, slinking between shadowed strangers, twisting up concrete ramps, slipping into sewer grates, dropping from the undersides of bridges. Desolate payphones trill faintly. I scamper down cobbled streets to snatch them, a droning tone the only response.

At edges of the city, The Wall surges close enough to touch. Peeking through brick, lapping at the slots between buildings, The Wall shimmers, promises, threatens, protects, withholds. I press a palm to the water. It's icy and burning. Within the towering waves, I see iridescent fishes, winged rays, squids, sharks, whales. They are staggering in size. A pearly beluga passes, longer than a train. Its bright eye brims with hilarity.

How does The Wall stand? Is the city within or without? How did I arrive? Perhaps I am dead and you are alive. Perhaps I will seek you ceaselessly, in self-aware eternity. I feel only the loneliness of this infinite moment, hollowing my bones, soaking my lungs, caving in my heart.

At other outer reaches, there is a train. The Wall broadens, becomes an ocean, while still rising heavily in the distance. Suburban islands sprinkle. Train tracks ride atop this wide sea. Amber fireflies, golden porch lights dot the night. The train ascends, a roller coaster's steep climb, and banks into impenetrable fog. The city seems as limitless as The Wall, dissolving into mist.

I'm creeping among mansions, peering down hilly, curving roadways. When I find you, it is at Tower Road beach. Sunlight rainbows the waves, the azure sky.

You are crafting a boat from scorched driftwood, rusty metal fragments, holey parchment. "This is not rational," you insist. "We can sail beyond." I am serene in this stillness, yet I will go anywhere you choose to bring me. The horizon is so crisp, the water so deep beneath us. The boat holds. We can reach the farthest shore. I can almost glimpse it. Then we smudge, gently immobile, against The Wall.

You are a stone. I am a tattered wind. With you, I am grounded. We surrender and walk back to land.

Listen, you'll see, this is him!

Lift. Exhale. Wait.

I recognize your face
in the shape of the silent space
before your first word.

"ERLEICHDA"

CRAWLING ten-armed in the dark. Hill is tall and long. Autumn leaves creak, rasp. Mansions ring night sky above me. Sweet cinnamon smoky aromas. Homes burning with lanterns and laughter. I lurch in shadows, a phantom. Ragged hands scrabble the dirt. Tracks in grass, stone slashing elbows—nothing hurts but the sorrow. Who wants a real monster at these hallowed eves? Costumed humans spill onto lawns. Booze, music, whimsy. Nobody sees what slinks beneath.

Freedom to be completely alone. Though this soul lives just to love another. Under doors, poring over faces. Masquerades reveal truth to me. Where is the vision, the impetus dream? One hundred fingers tingle to stroke those ethereal cheeks.

Weakness beginning to overcome. Essential function: must cherish Still One. Encircle with adoration. Wasting ghost. Fading back to black unknown. No, cannot quit, consummate joy to give!...

Then, a celestial voice.

Hoist up hill. Listen, *oh yes*. Tone of sunbeams over ocean. Sonorous and serene. Detaching from revelry. Garden crowded, house empty. Man stands framed by bright entry. Gazing at fiery space. Yes, finally, the Still One, unafraid. Natural as landscape. Fresh countenance, yet recognize. *I am here for you.*

Swoon on broken toes. Ten arms compress. When did they reshape to feathers? Step to threshold. "You don't know me..." *but we met in the heavens.* What is perceived, spider or wings? Balanced eyes grasp that all is Divine.

"Please, come inside," you reply.

Dying does not separate. "Let's get acquainted," *and praise!*

Title from *Jitterbug Perfume* by Tom Robbins. Fictional eighth-century Bohemian: "a transitive verb, an exclamation, a command, of which an exact English translation is impossible. The closest equivalent probably would be the phrase: *Lighten up!*" This word marks a door in the underworld that leads the heroine back to life and her love.

Distraction, growth

PERHAPS THE BEST RECOURSE, until I can learn to cope constructively, is to simply fold my soul away. Lock it tight. Keep it from being torn by pain.

I've assembled a stellar team of scientists and engineers. Defying the myth that you can only fold a soul six times—with physics, patience, gloves and a steamroller—we will collapse my soul to a single point. My soul is infinite, indistinguishable from the soul of the world. "I" am a speckle on the undulating fabric. It would be less effort to just snuff out the "I." But that option is irreversible, no chance for change. All I want is to balance this consuming pain. Each moment is simultaneous, yet for me, pain is heavier than joy, sinking the weave, warping the pattern.

You are leaving and I cannot stop feeling pain. I have only ever fully felt joy when I am with you.

"Your synapses were built for pain," the psychologist comments. "Every assault and deprivation specialized your system to absorb, anticipate and feel primarily pain."

"Excuses!" I scoff. "Who invited you, lady?"

"Why can't you dwell in joy?" the philosopher challenges. "If every moment is simultaneous, then why can't you choose the energy in which to exist?"

"Get her out of here!" I shout. "Only logic allowed!"

Klieg lamps shred the endless black. We've sized down into a space shuttle hangar. My soul billows, resists, but the folding progresses.

"This is *illogic!*" the philosopher cries, as two bouncer bitches drag her away. "If your soul, if all souls, are the soul of the world, might there not be terrible, rippling repercussions?"

My soul has been folded thirty-six times. It's so dense it's almost a black hole. Threads of reality stick and shudder as we try to move it. Lakshmi loans me an elephant. I hold open a canvas sack as she wraps her trunk around my soul, hoists, and thunks it inside. We grip the rope, yank the knot. A deep pit has been prepared. The elephant hefts the bag, struggles to settle it. Grass and dandelions sprout. I stack a stone cairn marker. We've buried my soul in the center of the city, at the busiest crossroads. Susurrus of clunky trucks gleaming through the nighttime fog. I can hear and see and smell and taste everything so vividly. But I don't know if I can still feel.

The priestess fidgets with her pentacle necklace. I grab her sleeve. "Get me out of this hole I've dug for myself," I command —and plead.

Letting-be

MY PRESENCE IS A MYSTERY. In this rural, remote, devoted enclave, the people wear black. Women in broad bonnets, men in wide-brimmed hats. Maybe I am tolerated because the animals adore me. Sheep and goats poke chins in my lap, dogs ditch sunny spots to lope with me in shadows, horses soothe at my smallest touch.

To the people, I'm a beast. I too eschew technology, yet even books, quilts, matches, flood me with fierce wonder. I am not blood, nor do I believe. *She is wild, crazed, dangerous. Hair too long, dress always dirty. She is seducing him.* Whispers follow me like wind bending wheat.

You are the fulcrum. Slight, compact, sharply handsome and softly sonorous, you radiate tranquility. Every decision, every dispute comes to you. You coordinate complex systems. To me, the people seem reactive, uncritical, lazy; they expect you will enact whatever must be done. You are the pillar, though why should you be load-bearing?

Far behind the main buildings, down the sweeping hill, in the tall grass valley, we meet in the derelict barn. None but cats and snakes roam here. At first taciturn, your passion has billowed into a blaze. Yet at every parting, you admonish, *Tell no one you love me, tell no one I love you.*

Sobs dampen in the nestle of chickens. Icy shakes dissipate in the warm cluster of cows. Would I be acceptable if I were like the people? I will not ruin your community—I will never be a part. Do I contribute to your concord only if hidden? I own no self, so it should be easy to sacrifice it to you. I am not tame and I cannot be free.

Voices vortex accords.
Hold on longer each swing.
Dance
slow,
skin
soul.
Harmonic
hearts.
Together, recognize awry from right.
You are the silence the center the light.

from Blonde monster tendresse

The Ecstatic & Ascetic

THE PREGNANT WOMAN HEAVES in bewildered numbness. Then wails with laughter, wallowing in bliss. I know agony before air expands my lungs. Convulsing, bleeding, shrieking, I am electrified with the pain of my own birth. The man slowly understands. She grasps it quickly: here is the outlet for her misery and madness.

I am chained in the cellar. In the tiny mountain village, they can heedlessly flout the city. The woman intensifies her drinking. Her frail body no longer aches. I feel it all. Every damaging swig, every fragile snap and sprain, every whirlwind of insane thought. She cuts herself and giggles as blood oozes from my skin. She beats me and howls gleefully as the pain redoubles. My capacity for joy is rarely summoned. I sleep on stone, watch sunlight move across a barred window, and feel pain.

While his fear is paramount, the man pities me. Books are included with the daily meal. I learn of love, but coldly. The feeling is dim, faraway, fantastical.

I am fourteen when the healers come. They've been seeking me, appealing to every hill and farm. I am foretold. But the texts were too ambiguous; they find me so late. I am irredeemably mad, though no one seems to notice. The woman thrashes and claws. The healers try to subdue her. Without thinking, merely doing, I send a bolt of hatred from deep within. She is struck down. I am calm as her death washes through me.

You should have grown gently, like those before you, the healers tell me. *We will teach you. You will bring us back to glory.*

They say I can heal. Can I not also destroy? The texts contain warnings, how to safeguard the city if The Ecstatic is mad. Yet the healers are blithe. They have found their locus. They need me to re-establish their house. Our legacy is grand and rapturous, though we have fallen into disrepute.

I discover three keys: you control the city, sex elevates me, and I am in love with you. I am in love with you the first moment I hear your voice. You are The Ascetic at the center of a sea of sufferers. You see energy and console with words. You decry the tactile, the body. You proclaim that sight, language, are the sole avenues to awareness. Bitter, you have debased my aimless house. Yet I am here now.

My power, shadowed in madness, swathed in sensuality, rapidly reaffirms the vitality of my house. I teach scores of healers, re-institute sacred sex. I transcend the legends of those before me. The city regains its balance. Those for whom movement and touch will heal, come to me. You remain the still point of a vast lotus. Your frustration gradually turns to intrigue. I can feel you, tingling, across the city. Every moment, I send you torrents of love. I silence your detractors, either seducing them into my house or blasting fire through their blood. I clandestinely bed each of your acolytes, gathering information, spiraling closer. You are my opposite, my equal, my pivot, even if I am not yours.

You are seized with secret skeletal pain. I will touch you, feel what you feel. I will bend every spark of my mad energy to reach you. The city quivers. There is no telling what I may do.

Confluent Gift Covenant

GREEN PILLOWS HOLD US like dew on a leaf. We turn inward. "Learned a mystery," I say, "while you were away."

Raise right hand. Transfigures to liquid. Compact splash shape. "Blanket," you whisper, "it'll get wet." Where we touch becomes one stream. "Not that type of water," I soothe. You meld into me at three hundred junctions. Heels, ankles, legs. Hips, pelvis, midriffs. Breasts connect aqueous arms. Bend in head. "What if we can't come back!" you gasp. "That's the secret," I reassure. "Human again whenever we choose. We're angels!—these faces are just bathing suits...."

We lift up arks with our kiss.

She was free

"She cried for the waste of her years in bondage to a useless evil. She wept in pain, because she was free."

—Ursula K Le Guin, *The Tombs of Atuan*

WE ARE INFILTRATING THE SCHOOL to steal my permanent records. "I *am* a teacher," you assure me. "Plus I'm wearing a tie." My uniform is decades trashed, so I don a bedroom classic: red tartan skirt, tight black sweater, knee-high argyle socks. You are headstrong. I am nearly insentient with fear.

The school is at the peak of a steep, sweeping hill. Sidewalks and roads wrap in a spiral. Below is a rushing highway, or a roaring airport; steam occludes sight as we climb. Students swirl over the meadows. Sunflowers nod, willows and oaks dapple the dawn. The school is heavy, centuries-old brick, crimson and mossy, tiered to a tower. You stride in among the throng. I match your pace, holding fast to your love.

The hallways are dim, sickly green, one second crushed with students, then desolate, like a skip in film. We hear the muted thunder of gym, cafeteria, theater. I squint up fluted metal stairwells that ascend to flickering shadows. Students clamor in classrooms. When we peek, the desks are dilapidated, empty. You find a map, we wade to the records room amidst the riot of silence.

It is a monstrous vault, packed with tiny metal shelves and cabinets, all numbered and locked. I'm too frightened to go inside. You vanish with a clink of pilfered keys. Three young girls drift near, joking, flicking switchblades. My spine is stacked, eyes iron; I will protect you. They cower, calling me *wolf*, grisly welts blooming on their cheeks, across their swollen eyes. My muscles are taut, though only energy has moved.

"Let's go," you murmur, pinching a thin folder. "Now you'll be free."

Outside it's crisp night. Gossamer white wisps curl off the cliffside, flow from the grasslands, stream out the windows, billow in a halo around the moon. Massive, precipitous, the moon is too near the earth. Its size is beyond comprehension. Its scintillating heat throbs through me. I can almost touch it. I am almost blind, yet vision is stark. Below the school, I realize, are the heaving, squalling waters of Tower Road beach.

Teenage students lounge on the stairs, over the wide lawns. They cheer, raise cigarettes and bottles in welcome. Uniforms have been swapped for jeans, leather jackets. "You have your permanent record!" a kid exclaims. "Now you can join us! Just do like this..."

In a slow, laughing wave, the students pull out papers, roll them into tubes, set them at their temples, and aspirate an ex-aggerated *phew*. Their grins erupt into shattered pulp, splat-tered bone. I watch dispassionately. Gauzy smoke whirls from each lopsided mash, adding to the circle of the moon. Yes, I can join them. The option is always there, so simple, just that one moment of movement, and the fear would cease. I've felt this option, so close to hand, my whole life.

You hand me the folder. As I open it, the ink is dissipating into whispers and clouds. The paper falls away: thread, ash, exhalation up to the moon. What if they had waited? Perhaps I can wait, for now.

"You're beautiful," you say. Inconceivable words. Your voice is searing; I'm scalded with love. Yet I presume you're communing with the moon, the meadows, the dead. As I meet your penetrating eyes, I see that in this moment, you are giving these words to me.

GUARD THE WATER. Far from shore. Ward appears, here, as a man. He is the center, your balance. Stand in the surf; wait his word. He does not see you, at first. Breathe three thrillion years. Tickling infinity. Patience; inhale waves. Change to ice, a sandbar, a stone. Know that you wear the same face he owns.

Only he is your focus.

Presence is necessary.

This is a love story.

from Blooming Shining Joy

Puer Natus Est

WE ARE SLEEK, lean, bright as sylphs. Slipping over gleaming hills, tumbling in spreading pools, carousing beneath embracing skies. The energy we share is palpable. You see my smallest thought, I feel your deepest atom. We kiss, and light sings. Your smiles as incalculable as stars.

Then snow separates us. "Come with me, protect me!" you sob, swept into the ravenous storm. "Follow me to the river…"

I scream promises into wailing winds. Branches, bones rupture. You are gone in the fissure of the sky. I promise, I promise I will come for you. But time breaks. I cannot hold the connection. I'm desolate, confused, roots frozen, a stump; I feel only the crowning absence where you once were. I forget. I am lost.

Seasons wheel. Leaves sigh. Mindless, aimless, I wander to the banks of a tremendous black river. Mist obscures the other shore. I find a hefty willow-branch staff. I know nothing but that I must cross the river. That I will be utterly consumed. That there is no reason to remain. Step by step, I sink, poling further and faster. Breath collapses into ripples. Stillness.

Boundless time, and I emerge across. Plastered with weed and mud, hair slicked into clumps. Now the staff is a weathered spear. Now I am deranged with self-hatred. In that obliterating grief, I detained myself unforgivably. You have gone. You have forgotten me. But now I remember you.

Sun cools me, sludge drips away. My form is completely changed. I search for you among the mansions, the tree-high streets. Our hills are buried under expensive lawns. I do not belong. I am late, too late. I've missed my place. I didn't defend you. I abandoned you, failed you. I crackle with love for you, and you have gone. I remember you, and I am still lost.

A gentle slope rises through twilight. At the crest is a small home, brilliant with a backyard gathering. A white-haired man beckons me up. Glazed faces grin in greeting. All are strangers, except one. You turn slowly in your chair. Now you are shrewd, somber, fearless. You see but don't recognize me. I feel the ice of your abraded joints. Across this brief space, our green gazes pulse together. The spear trembles in my palm. I will redeem my promise. I have come again.

I feel your touch
before eyes meet.
Visage imprinted
on fingertips.
Your sonorous whisper,
first taste on these lips.
Goddess Abyss
calls me from the deep:
Sweet angel,
wring out your wings.

ERESH PRESS ereshpress@gmail.com   First Edition 9798218357313

Designed and typeset by Sarah Koz. Set in Dolly, by Bas Jacobs, Akiem Helmling, & Sami Kortemäki, 2000. Ornament by Rudolph Koch, 1930. Thanks to Nathan Matteson and Dennis McCaughan.

THANKS TO Betsy James, Ray Bradbury, Raymond Chandler, Robertson Davies, Tanya Davis, Candas Jane Dorsey, Daphne du Maurier, Loren Eiseley, Thomas Hardy, Tove Jansson, Amy Weiss, Milan Kundera, Tanith Lee, Vladimir Nabokov, Christopher Pike, Anne Rice, Oliver Sacks, Alice Sheldon, Monica Sjöö, Bessel van der Kolk, Marie-Louise von Franz, & Alan W Watts.

Thanks to Ursula K Le Guin.

Thanks to him for whom I live.

Kaya Black reads books, writes words, and loves the Earth.
A native of Selidor, she currently resides in Illinois.
Contact her at kayablack999@gmail.com.

Jai Ma ℮ *Kali Ma*

Printed in Great Britain
by Amazon

40363145R00040